THE OTHERS

BY

SCOTT JACKSON

Scott Jackson

KING'S WAY PRESS

King's Way Press
4215 Jimmy Lee Smith Pkwy Suite 19-210
Hiram, GA 30141

Published and printed in the United States of America

First Publication June, 2019

ISBN 978-0-9988367-8-2

www.kwp-books.com

Cover Artwork Copyright © 2019 by Zach McCain

Interior Design by Zombie Book Design

THE OTHERS

BY

SCOTT JACKSON

A CHILLY auTUMn WInD BLEW tHROUGH tHE CEMEtERY, whistling softly between the marble headstones, combining with the underlying, subtle sounds of nature to create a grand symphony of the harvest season. Leaves whispered as they stirred and whirled softly upon the ground, dancing in the gentle breeze. Fall embraced the graveyard in a gentle caress; impatient lovers embracing after a long absence.

Jack ambled among the garden of grave markers, aimlessly tarrying among the dead, occasionally reading the inscriptions to see whom among those commemorated upon the polished faces he might know. He was alone among the dead; not a living soul to be found among these silent monuments to the dearly departed. No sound, outside of that of nature, encroached upon his serene solitude.

I suppose I'd better venture forward, he thought, reluctant to leave the comfortable quietness of the cemetery. *I wouldn't want to be caught here by those frightful creatures that sometimes lurk in this place.*

Darkness was beginning to descend like a heavy curtain in slow motion. Soon, the landscape would be shrouded in deep, inky darkness; the silvery moon hanging in the night sky the only source of light. Already the amber glow of the setting sun began to recede into deeper shades of twilight. Soon, the polished marble headstones would reflect the light of the moon; gleaming and glowing with otherworldly luminescence.

Jack was unsettled and nervous about this all important mission. Not at all the adventurous sort by nature, this assignment was far outside of his comfort zone. Apprehension causing him to falter, he lingered among the dead far longer than necessary.

I'm not even sure why I was chosen for this mission, he pondered, sighing deeply. *Still, I have a job to do and I'll do it as best I can.*

Slowly, he shuffled toward the ancient, heavy, rust encrusted, inward-leaning gates of the graveyard entrance, reluctance weighing on him like a two-ton boat anchor. His knees shook and creaked, his teeth chattered loudly. The chill in the air bearing no responsibility for either; his sense of dread and impending doom the true cause for his discomfort. Sighing inwardly, he summoned up a reserve of courage and headed for the ancient gates.

■■

Since it's Halloween, there's sure to be many, many more of them out than normal.

It was true.

The creatures, while always lurking about, were always out in far greater numbers on this hallowed night of nights. The evening air was pregnant with mystique, uncertainty, and hidden dangers. A current ran through the air, unseen; electricity zipping through an invisible conduit. Anticipation and fear threatened to overtake his stalwart determination.

Nevertheless Jack moved on.

Passing through the decrepit iron gates, he froze in place as he heard it. Faint at first, but growing ever closer, louder by the second. The sound striking terror deep within his bones. His very marrow freezing solid inside the outer shells of white.

It's them…the others!

Swallowing his fear and fighting the urge to turn and flee toward home, he instead dashed for the safety of a towering, nearby oak tree. He hid behind the huge base of tree, trembling with terror, as the cacophony of sounds reached a crescendo. Abruptly, the noises ceased, as if the mute button on a celestial remote control had suddenly been pressed. Only the soft sounds of nature's never-ending chorus remained audible. Several tense seconds passed, Jack feeling the creepy, crawly sensation of someone...or *something* watching him.

"We see you there. You can come out from behind that tree!"

The voice startled him at first. However, it certainly sounded friendly enough. It definitely wasn't the hostile, monstrous voice he'd have expected of one of *the others*. Knees knocking, he debated internally for several seconds before cautiously peering around the base of the oak. A small thrill of delight traveled up his spine and through his bones as he realized that he'd been wrong.

*It wasn't **them** after all*, he thought, an immense wave of relief washing over him.

Tension melting away like ice on hot asphalt, he loosed a deep, whooshing sigh of relief. Walking out from behind the tree, he hailed the small group huddled together on the sidewalk. A diverse group of beings stood side by side, just a dozen feet away from his hiding place. An assorted assembly that included a witch, a goblin, and a zombie; all waiting patiently for him to engage them.

"Hello, I'm Jack," he stated, relieved to have found suitable traveling companions in this dangerous, unfamiliar territory. He joined the small group on the sidewalk, questions threatening to spill from his mouth in rapid fire succession.

"Hi Jack, I'm Carly," the witch said. Pointing to the zombie, she continued, "That's my brother, Kyle."

"And, I'm Carson," the goblin stated.

"Are you guys on a mission too?" Jack asked.

"Yeah," Kyle responded with glee. "A mission to take as much candy as possible tonight!"

"You betcha!" Carson enthusiastically agreed.

"I'm on a scouting mission."

"Is that something you can do while going door to door with us?" Carly asked.

Jack took a moment to ponder this question. While going "door to door" sounded a little bolder than the more subtle approach he'd intended, it'd probably accomplish exactly what he'd been sent here to do.

Besides, there's safety in numbers, he thought.

*I'll probably be safer with my new friends if we happen upon a group of **them.*** He shuddered at the thought, fighting to keep from visibly trembling in front of his newfound companions.

"Sure," he finally answered. "Let's go."

■■■

Friendship newly minted, the group resumed strolling down the sidewalk again, Carly leading the way. As they made their way past several darkened houses, Jack had occasion to get a closer look at his disparate traveling companions. Each of them were unique; all of them seemingly at ease with the presences of each other.

Funny, he thought. *I've always been under the impression that goblins and zombies vehemently hated each other. That's the conventional wisdom anyway.*

Kyle and Carson seemed more like best friends; not at all the relationship he would've expected.

Well, not everything you hear is true, I guess.

He also noticed that all three, the witch, the goblin, and the zombie, were swinging in their right hands what appeared to be hollowed out pumpkins, made of some kind of hardened, inorganic material. He was tempted to ask what these strange jack o' lanterns were for, but he supposed he'd find out soon enough. He didn't want to make his newfound friends uncomfortable by asking them too many personal questions this early on.

As they approached a large, three-story house that was decorated with oversized spiders, fearsome jack o' lanterns, uncarved pumpkins, witches, and orange, brightly flashing lights, Jack's marrow again froze in his bones. Directly ahead of them on the sidewalk, approaching from the opposite direction, was a group of five beings rapidly closing the distance between them. At least two of this group appeared to be *the others!* The sight was one that nearly caused his trembling legs to lock up, and he almost stumbled.

It's them, he thought, panic threatening to overtake him. The group heading toward them, on a collision course, was comprised of a fearsome werewolf, a vampire with blood trailing from its ruby-red lips, and a blood encrusted, headless ghoul. These, he wasn't frightened of in the least. It was *the others*…two of the most terrifying creatures he'd ever laid eyes upon, walking just few feet behind the monsters. Their appearances were both frighteningly hideous and thoroughly nauseating. If he were capable of such, he'd have vomited for sure. His traveling companions noticed his discomfort, immediately setting about offering their comforting support and words of encouragement.

"Oh, don't worry about them," Carson offered. "They're not that scary…and they won't hurt you."

"Yeah," Carly said. "They're here for the same reason we are. They won't hurt you. In fact, I know her," she said pointing to the vampire. "Hey Deborah," she called out to the female vampire.

"Oh, hey!" the vampire replied. "Look, Kendall, it's Carly, Carson, and Kyle," she said to the werewolf. In response, the werewolf growled ferociously and waved a large, furry paw toward the group.

"It's not th-the-them I'm worried about," Jack stuttered.

"Dude, what's wrong with you?" Kyle asked.

"It's them!" Jack stated, pointing to the two terrifying creatures who were striding ever closer to them.

He nearly fainted at their appearance. One was a tall mass of pale, lumpy flesh, with a doughy complexion and long neck. The other was darker but no less appalling to behold. Masses of lumpy, gooey flesh, covered with fine hair that encompassed their entire bodies…they sported even more, thicker, much longer hair growing from atop their heads. One of the horrifying duo sporting thick, braided black hair that cascaded half-way down its back. They resembled skeletons that someone with a twisted imagination had used clay to mold horrific, flaccid visages around. Their appearances were far worse than anything he'd ever imagined.

Not comprehending who Jack was pointing to, Carly encouraged him to move on. "Come on Jack, no one's going to hurt you. This is Halloween. It's all in good fun."

"And, it's all about looting as much candy as possible," Kyle chimed in.

Carson grunted his agreement. "Come on guys, let's get going. We still have a lot of houses left to hit tonight!"

He looked over toward Jack who was obviously still reluctant to move. "Man, what're you gonna put your candy in?"

Still eyeing the approaching monstrosities warily, Jack didn't comprehend the odd question. Before he could consider it further, Carson brought out a large, white plastic shopping bag from inside his jack o' lantern.

"Glad I came prepared," he said. "I brought these extra bags along in case my pumpkin gets full. I guess, I can spare one." He handed one of the bags to Jack. "Here, take this."

Jack took the bag, still unsure as to what purpose it was supposed to serve.

Kyle studied Jack for a moment before asking, "Jack, have you ever been trick-or-treating before?"

"No," Jack answered honestly. "I have not."

"Well, that explains a lot," Carly stated. "Okay, here's the deal. People dress up as monsters, superheroes, ghouls, and creatures on Halloween. Then they go out and ring people's doorbells or knock on doors. They ask for candy and it gets put in here," she held up her jack o' lantern. "Got it?"

"So, they pay tribute to us with candy?" Jack asked.

"Pretty much dude. Let's go!" Carson exclaimed, pulling Jack by the arm toward the first house.

"Dr. Holcomb lives here and he gives out the most awesome goodie-bags!" Kyle exclaimed as he reached for the doorbell.

Following the lead of the others, Jack held forth his bag when the door opened and the others yelled, "Trick or treat!"

To his surprise, the terrifying creature, one of *the others*, who answered the door dropped a heavy pouch of candies and sweets into Jack's open bag. "Nice costumes!" the man said as he closed the door. "Happy Halloween!"

Jack trembled with fear, unable to speak or move, until *the other's* frightening visage was finally blocked out by the closing door. He'd been rooted to the ground as *the other* had stood within a couple of feet of him.

"Happy Halloween!" Jack's companions all replied enthusiastically.

■■

There was much about his new companions that Jack didn't quite understand. Not the least of which was this ritualistic collection of candy. *The others* answering their doors didn't seem the least bit afraid of the vampires, witches, goblins, zombies, and ghouls. Likewise, the monsters didn't seem the least bit intimidated by *the others* who handed out the candy either.

Maybe there's hope yet.

Jack supposed that he would continue on with his companions for as long as possible. Already his bag of candy hung low and heavy, filled nearly to capacity with all manner of sweet surprises. While the method of carrying out his important mission was unorthodox, he supposed all that really mattered was that he complete it. He would then take the vital information he gathered back to share with his people.

■■

"Hey, Carly, Carson, Kyle," a voice rang out. "The party's about to begin. Bring your friend and come on."

"Who's that?" Kyle asked.

"I think that's Bridgette," Carly replied.

"She's supposed to be having an epic Halloween party," Carson stated.

"Well, let's go," Carly replied as she turned to Jack. "You coming with us?"

"Sure," Jack said hesitantly. He wasn't sure about entering one of the dwelling places of *the others*.

I'll just have to trust my friends. If a witch, a goblin, and a zombie, aren't afraid to enter this domicile, I should be safe there as well.

■■

Two hours later, the party began winding down, many of the attendees having gone home. Jack was confused by the odd behavior of his friends. They seemed to mimic the behaviors he would've expected of *the others*. They didn't act the way he'd expect such creatures to act. He also didn't understand why these monsters and creatures were having a party inside the living quarters of *the others*.

In fact, none of the party attendees acted in a manner consistent with their existence. It was all a little befuddling and confusing for Jack. He began to think it was time to take his leave and continue this mission on his own.

I'm not sure there's much more to be learned here, he thought. *I will regret, however, leaving my new friends behind.*

Jack hadn't made many friends, even among his own people. He'd always been considered a loner and had never bothered to do anything to disabuse his neighbors of that notion. Now that he'd made these wonderful new friends, he was reluctant to take leave of them.

I'll have to return their kindness by inviting them back to my home. Perhaps they'll visit after my mission is complete.

■■■

As Jack contemplated how to make a graceful departure from the party, Bridgette and Barbara, sisters who appeared to be zombie nurses, came back into the living room. Barbara suggested that they make some popcorn and watch some scary movies.

"Anyone who wants to hang out is welcome to stay," Barbara said.

"I'm out," a female troll named Jorie said, as she headed for the front door. "It's a school night. My parents will kill me if I'm out much later."

"Come on guys, I just ordered pizzas," Bridgette offered.

■■■

In the end, only Jack and his three companions were left in the living room with Bridgette and Barbara.

"Okay, I think we should remove our costumes and get comfortable," Bridgette said. "I'm going to take off my makeup now, anyone else coming?"

The girls went upstairs as a group, leaving the boys alone in the living room. As they exited up the stairs, Jack heard Barbara ask, "Who's the silent, brooding skeleton?"

"That's Jack. We just met him tonight. He seems like a nice guy. A little shy, I guess."…

■■■

"Okay guys," Kyle said, "I'm going to the bathroom to wash this stuff off, too."

"I'll go after you come back, then it'll be Jack's turn," Carson replied.

Jack didn't know what to make of these curious exchanges. He didn't know what Bridgette meant by "removing costumes and makeup". He decided he'd say goodbye as soon as they all returned to the living room. For now, he waited, seated with Carson on the couch.

"Where'd you get your costume?" Carson asked suddenly shattering the near deafening silence.

"What?" Jack asked. He'd been lost in thought and hadn't comprehended what Carson had asked.

"Where'd you get that costume? It's very realistic. Almost life-like."

"What's a costume?" Jack asked.

"Come on man," Carson replied. "Where'd you get the costume?"

Before Jack could answer, he heard the girls laughing and talking as they came back downstairs. When they turned the corner, coming into view, he was horrified by what he saw. The girls who'd gone upstairs as witches and zombies had now been transformed into horrible visages of pure terror.

They'd morphed into the very creatures that Jack had been sent here to spy upon! To his horror, he realized that they'd been in disguise the entire time. Gasping, he looked toward Carson, realization dawning on him that all of his newfound friends had been in what the boy had described as "costumes". What's worse, they believed that he was in costume as well.

They think I'm one of them, he thought, panic beginning to creep into his bones. Knees knocking together, he involuntarily shrank away from Carson, melting deeper into the couch cushions.

"What's wrong with you man? You look like you've seen a ghost," Carson queried, puzzled expression fixed upon his brow.

If I'd only seen a ghost…I wouldn't be too terrified to speak, Jack thought. Before he could answer, Kyle returned from the bathroom.

"Why's it so quiet in here?"

The sound of his voice commanded Jack's attention and glancing up from his place the couch, he once again recoiled in horror. This time, Jack heard the faint cracking of one of his rib bones as he pushed ever deeper into the back couch cushion. After removing his makeup and costume, Kyle became the most loathsome vision of all. Pasty white skin, dotted with small freckles; salt and pepper hair that belied his true age. Hawkish nose that came to a blunt point, upon which set a pair of wire-rimmed spectacles.

It was too much for Jack to take. In one abrupt lunge, he bolted upright from the couch, nearly knocking Bridgette over in the process. He made for the front door with the speed of a professional sprinter, leaving behind a group of puzzled kids.

As the front door slammed behind him, Bridgette rubbed the spot where Jack had elbowed her out of his way. "Man, that dude was bony," she remarked as she massaged her side. "Felt like his elbow was nothing but bone!"

A moment later, the front door banged open again as Callie and Kerry spilled inside, laughing at some unknown cause of mirth. "That guy was so weird," Kerry said between giggles.

"I know," Callie said. "I've never seen anyone scream and run off like that! Our costumes must be better than I thought they were."

Callie was dressed as an NFL cheerleader and Kerry donned a Superman costume. Her joke set the entire group to laughing.

"Nah, dude was freaking out before you two even showed up," Kyle said...

■■■

There he is. He's been hiding there all night. Probably waiting to make sure no one is in the graveyard.

From her vantage point, perched high above the ground on a thick branch of the ancient oak tree, Callie could see Jack cautiously appear from behind a small copse of trees just outside and to the left of the timeworn, iron cemetery gates. No one could see her where she sat hidden, high among the dense branches and remaining leaves on the massive oak tree which had stood as a silent sentry over the graveyard for the last one hundred-fifty years.

Now, let's see where he's going.

Even though she'd only caught a momentary glimpse of Jack before he'd made his hasty exit from the party, she knew right away that he was one of *the others.* It was something she could usually detect immediately.

She watched as he slowly made his way inside the decrepit gates of graveyard. He seemed to be heading toward the back, where the older graves and three large, rough-hewn, stone mausoleums waited. Sensing that it was safe to follow him undetected, Callie silently leapt down from the tree in one fluid motion, knowing that for a mere mortal, such a feat would have broken both their legs. She landed with such grace as to make the lithest feline jealous.

Using the bigger marble monuments for cover, she followed Jack to the farthest reaches of the graveyard. She saw that he was headed for the largest of the three stone buildings. Her curiosity piqued, she continued her stealthy approach and surveillance. Jack entered the building after throwing a cursory glance over his shoulder to ensure no one else was around or watching. Callie darted behind an ancient tombstone, just barely in time to avoid being seen.

Pausing for a few seconds after Jack entered the tomb, she cautiously made her approach, eyes locked on the entrance in case he made a sudden reappearance. Once she'd made it to the side of the building, she quickly proceeded to the doorway. She peered inside, standing just to the left of the open entrance. At first glance, it appeared that Jack was kneeling down behind a large granite vault that sat slightly askew in the center of the room. Only his head and shoulders were visible. As she watched, even those body parts disappeared suddenly.

Then it hit her.

He's not kneeling. He's disappeared down some kind of hidden staircase!

Debating whether to follow, and how long to wait before doing so, she heard a sudden, ever so slight, scraping sound as the vault in the center of the room righted itself. Callie rushed into the room, only to find the vault was now covering whatever subterranean staircase that was hidden under it.

There must be a secret switch somewhere that operates the vault, sliding it out of the way.

She looked around the room, not seeing anything that immediately stood out as a possible means of activating the sliding vault. Along each side and the back wall of the crypt were rows of brass name placards. There were columns of these markers four high, and six wide on each wall. Behind each placard, and the stone it was embedded in, lay the remains of someone in the Astor family. Callie carefully felt along each wall, around and over each brass plate, seeking something, anything, that could be used to operate the sliding vault.

I could smash that vault pretty easily, she thought.

Caution kept her from doing so.

I don't know who, or how many creatures lie beyond that hidden staircase. I should probably just report what I've seen. The council can decide what to do about it.

She decided not to risk going further on her own. There was no telling where Jack was going or why he'd ventured from wherever he came from in the first place.

Besides, the sun will be coming up soon. My sunscreen will need to be reapplied. My own assignment among these mortals will be over soon enough, she thought to herself as she exited the mausoleum.

Smiling as she fondly thought of home and her family that awaited her there, Callie's upper lip curled back just slightly enough that the witch, watching from her hidden place on top of the stone structure, could see her elongated canines glinting as they reflected the glow of the waning moonlight.

She's one of the others!

The witch shrank down as low as she could get to the rooftop, fearful of being seen. Her flesh pimpled with goosebumps, a shiver traveled up her spine. The very thought of *the others* was enough to cause her joints to lock up with fright. Actually seeing one with her own eyes had been worse than she'd ever feared. As she watched Callie disappear from sight, the witch hoped she never encountered one of *the others* again!

■■■

Standing before the council of The Brotherhood of The Bones, Jack neared the end of the delivery of his oral report regarding *the others*. He'd never been one who was comfortable with speaking in front of large groups. There were several thousand of his kind in attendance tonight, anxiously awaiting his final proclamation.

"In summing up, I can't recommend making our existence known yet. *The others* are just too odd. Too unpredictable. Too different. I don't think they would handle the knowledge that we exist very well."

A murmur of disappointment arose from the crowd. Prior to beginning his task, Jack had shared his kinsmen's hope that the report he would ultimately give would be a positive one. That they were finally going to be able to reveal themselves to *the others* and possibly coexist in peace. Alas, he now feared that day would never come.

At least, probably not in my lifetime, Jack mused.

"I cannot recommend that we reveal ourselves yet. Maybe the next time we venture forth, things will have changed. That's our best hope for now."

As he stepped away from the podium, the air of disappointment clouding the auditorium was palpable. He shook a few hands as he dismounted the speaking platform. All he really wanted to do right now was to go home to his family and get some much needed rest. He'd had a stressful adventure to say the least...

THE END

ABOUT THE AUTHOR:

Scott Jackson is a former naval intelligence officer, now retired, although still working in the field as an independent contractor.

The Others is his first venture into the writing world, but he's already working on other titles, with *Social*, a novel soon to be published by King's Way Press. Additionally he's working on several other writing projects, including a collection of Halloween themed short stories and a Halloween novella.

Scott currently resides in the Great Smoky Mountains region with his wife, his two children, and their many pets. Trout fishing is one of his many outdoor passions.

Be sure to keep an eye out for future offerings from this rising star in the literary world!

www.ingramcontent.com/pod-product-compliance
Lightning Source LLC
Chambersburg PA
CBHW050921120626
46552CB00004B/1697